ICE CREAM FOR BREAKFAST

by Betty Jo Schuler

illustrated by Estella Hickman

For my husband Paul G.
for believing in me

PAGES™

Third printing by Willowisp Press 1997.

Published by Willowisp Press
801 94th Avenue North, St. Petersburg, Florida 33702

Printed in the United States of America

4 6 8 10 9 7 5 3

ISBN 0-87406-578-X

Contents

1. A Weird Place to Live 5

2. What a Mixed-up Day at School! .. 11

3. Zippers in the Back 19

4. Disaster at the Movies! 27

5. Dad's Run-in with
Messy Doughnuts 31

6. Everybody Keeps Staring 37

7. Upside-down Cake 43

DRAWKCAB

A Weird Place to Live

"Look! Those people are walking backward," said Liz Myers. She pointed out the window of the van.

Her brother Mark looked out the window, too. "Weird," he said.

"This whole town is weird," Liz said. "Even the name."

Mark nodded. His sister was right. Drawkcab was a strange name for a town.

"Here's where we turn," Dad said.

"Are you sure?" Mom asked. "I thought the house Uncle Bert left us was on Miami Street. That sign says 'IMAIM.'"

Dad glanced at the sign in the rear view mirror. "It looks like Miami to me," he said.

He pulled around the corner and parked the van. "This should be the place, all right," he said. He pointed to a house across from the van.

Everyone climbed out to take a look.

"Something's wrong here," Mom

whispered. "Look! The houses all face the wrong way. The back yards are in the front."

The Myers family stared at the row of neatly fenced yards. Each had a brightly colored trash can sitting near the road. Some had swimming pools. Some had barbecue grills. Some had sandboxes for little kids to play in. A few had dog houses.

"Hey," said Mark, "if the back yards are in front, then the front yards must be in back. That means the back doors are really the front doors. And the front doors are really the back doors."

Liz giggled. "No wonder those people were walking backward. Everything in this town is all turned around."

"Yeah!" said Mark. "I bet that's what Drawkcab means! It's 'backward' spelled backward!"

Mom and Dad sighed. But Mark and Liz ran through the gate into their new yard.

"Look at me," said Mark. He was running backward.

"I can do that," said Liz.

They both kept falling down. But they kept getting up again. And they were laughing as hard as they could.

What a Mixed-up Day at School!

The children in Drawkcab went to school from Friday to Monday. Mark and Liz thought that sounded great, but their first day was terrible.

The kids all walked backward. They even wore their clothes backward. Shirts and skirts were turned the wrong way. Hip pockets and wallets were in front. Necklaces were in back. Shoe laces were tied behind the ankle.

"It's hard to tell which way everyone is going," Liz said. "I'm getting dizzy."

"I'm getting mixed up," said Mark. "The principal said our classroom is the third one on the right. I don't know if that's going backward or forward."

Mark and Liz moved frontward and counted rooms backward. At last, they found the right door.

They stopped in the doorway. The teacher was sitting at her desk. Her back was turned to the class.

"Come in," she said. "There are just two seats left."

"How does she know we're here?" Mark whispered.

"Maybe she has eyes in the back of her head," Liz said.

"Time to say our ZYX's," said the teacher.

The class said the alphabet backward. Then the children counted from 100 to 0. They named the days from Sunday to Monday. They wrote the months from December to January.

Everything was done the wrong way for Mark and Liz. They couldn't get anything right. The other kids laughed at them behind their books. It was like that all day.

Time passed slowly. Both of the Myers children were glad when it was time to leave.

They practiced walking backward on the way home. They ran into each other and landed in a heap at their front door.

"Forget that!" said Liz. She was huffing and puffing from trying so hard.

"We can't," said Mark. "We have to learn."

They tried walking backward a few more times, and then gave up and tried some homework instead. That seemed easier.

"Dinner's ready!" called Mom a few hours later. She set apple pie and chocolate milkshakes on the table.

"What's this?" asked Dad. "Dessert first?"

"Everyone has dessert first in Drawkcab, dear. I learned that at the tekram today."

"At the what?"

"At the corner tekram," said Mom. "That's backward for market. I figured that out on my own."

"Great," said Liz and Mark. And they gobbled down their desserts.

When they were all done, Mom set the rest of the meal on the table. She served chicken, potatoes and broccoli.

Liz held her stomach. “Mom, I can’t eat broccoli when I’m full of pie and milkshakes.”

“You’ll learn,” her mother said. “We all will.”

Zippers in the Back

The second day at school was even worse. It was rainy to start with. Everyone seemed a little grouchy. And Mom served ice cream for breakfast. It was good, but Mark and Liz thought it was strange.

Then, before they left the house, Liz found out that she couldn't button her raincoat up the back without help. She asked Mark to give her a hand. She wanted to look like the other girls she had seen at school.

But when she got to school, she couldn't get the raincoat off. She had to wear it all day. The sun came out, and the day grew hot. So did Liz. Everyone stared at her, and she felt like a jerk. A very hot jerk.

Mark fell and hurt his backside trying to run backward in myg. The other boys laughed and pointed over their shoulders at him. Mark's face turned as red as his gym shorts.

"Going to this school isn't much fun," Liz said to her brother when they were going home.

Mark agreed.

The third day was no better.

Liz lost her hot dog trying to walk backward with her lunch tray. It slipped off her tray and rolled away. All she had left to eat was an apple.

Her stomach growled all afternoon. The kids sitting close to her heard it and giggled.

Mark got an *F* on a htam test because he had a hard time subtracting backward. He was really upset.

"I always earned *A*'s in math at our other school," he told Liz. "I never got an *F*."

"My hot dog never rolled under anyone's feet at the other school, either," she said.

When the Myers family sat down to eat that evening, Mark announced, "Mom and Dad, listen. We have to move. All of this backward stuff is awful."

Liz nodded. "Terrible. The only good part is being called Zil. I think Zil sounds better than Liz, don't you?"

"I think backward names are dumb," said Mark. He wasn't crazy about being called Kram.

"Not as dumb as wearing your clothes with the buttons the wrong way," said Liz. "How would you like to wear your raincoat all day?"

"How would you like to be a boy and have to wear your zippers in back?" Mark asked.

Liz grinned. "I guess things could be worse."

Dad shoved his cake away and reached for the roast. "This is ridiculous. I'm having dessert last, not first."

Mom sighed. "Maybe we should have stayed in Rightway."

Disaster at the Movies!

The Myers family needed cheering up. As soon as the weekend arrived, they all went to a movie at the Grand Movie House. The sign said "Esuoh Eivom Dnarg."

The movie was about a dog who got lost in a snow storm. The movie house manager ran the film backward, and the dog was found before he was lost. Mom said that spoiled the whole show.

But Liz and Mark thought parts of the movie were funny. They laughed like crazy when the dog ran backward up and down hills. Even Mom and Dad chuckled. But no one else in the theater laughed. They just stared at the Myers family.

At one point during the movie, Mom backed up the aisle to get some snacks. It was dark in the movie house, and she still had a lot of trouble walking backward. On her way she bumped into a little boy. She spilled his popcorn, and he started yelling. So did the little boy's father.

"What's the matter with you, lady?" he shouted. "Don't you even know how to walk?"

Liz and Mark were glad when it was time to go home. So were Mom and Dad.

Dad's Run-in with Messy Doughnuts

The whole family practiced walking backward the rest of the weekend. One minute they did all right. The next minute they looked like circus clowns. It was hard to tell if they were getting better or not.

They also tried to get used to wearing their clothes backward and eating dessert first. It wasn't easy, no matter what. Liz still struggled with reaching buttons in the back. Mark couldn't get the hang of tying his shoe laces behind his ankles. And dessert didn't seem special because it was always first.

They were so busy practicing everything that before they knew it, the weekend was over, and Mark and Liz were on their way to school again.

"Look, Liz," Mark said. "Isn't that Dad walking backward into the bakery—I mean, the yrekab?"

"It's him, all right," Liz said. "Oh, oh. He's going to miss the door..."

"...and walk into that fat lady who just came out!" Mark said. "And she has a big box!"

Liz took one look and closed her eyes tight. Besides the big box, the lady also had a big cat on a leash with her. Things didn't look good.

Crash! Dad backed into the fat lady. The box hit the sidewalk. Doughnuts rolled all over the place.

Jelly filling squirted out on the lady's left shoe. Cream filling squirted all over her right shoe. And a chocolate, nut-covered doughnut landed on her cat's back.

"MeeeOOWWWW!"

The cat yowled and hissed, and ran between Dad's legs. The leash got tangled around his ankles. He yelled right along with the cat. Then he slipped down, landing on his hands and knees.

Whack! The lady smashed a cream-filled doughnut on the back of Dad's

suit. He got up slowly. He wasn't hurt, but his face was as red as Mom's had been at the movie theater.

"Poor Dad," said Liz. She was trying hard not to giggle. "He gave up driving because he said it was impossible to move safely in reverse all the time. But it doesn't look like walking is very safe for him, either."

"I guess we're not the only ones with problems." Mark was laughing so hard he had to hold his sides.

"Yeah," said Liz. "I never thought parents could have the same troubles as we do."

"Maybe Dad and Mom should give up and walk frontward," said Liz.

"That might not be such a bad idea for all of us," Mark said.

Everybody Keeps Staring

"I just can't get the hang of walking backward," Liz complained the next day. "I wish I had eyes in the back of my head."

"I wish I was a potato with eyes all *over* my head," Mark said.

"I wish we didn't have to go to that dumb school," said Liz. "I'm tired of kids staring and laughing at me."

"Something has to be done," said Mark.

"But what?" asked Liz. "We can't change the whole school, or the whole town."

"Then we'll just have to be different," Mark said.

"You mean—be ourselves?" asked Liz. "Do things our own way?"

Mark grinned. "Exactly."

So both Mark and Liz walked to school frontward that day. They wore their clothes frontward, too. It felt so good that they both smiled all the way. They tried not to pay much attention to the people who pointed and stared.

“I don’t care if no one speaks to us,” said Liz.

“Hardly anyone talks to us, anyway,” said Mark.

They were walking up the steps of the school building when a pretty, blond-haired girl backed past them. The other day when the same girl passed, Liz had looked away. Liz knew the girl’s name, but she had looked away because she felt embarrassed. Liz had felt embarrassed because she still didn’t walk backward very well.

But today, Liz felt more like herself. She looked right at the girl. She gave her a huge smile.

The girl stopped and said, "Hi, Zil."

"My name is Liz. But hi, Patty."

The girl giggled. "My name's Yttap, but you can call me Patty if you like. Want to sit with me in the cafeteria today?"

"Sure!" Liz said. She was surprised and happy to be invited. "See you then."

Mark and Liz started down the hallway, but a red-haired boy called out and stopped them.

"Hi, Kram," the boy said. "You know something? Your shirt looks really cool that way."

Mark looked down at his buttons and grinned. "My name's Mark, but thanks. It's handy this way. You ought to try it sometime."

"Maybe I will," said the boy.

After class, their teacher stopped Liz and Mark in the hallway. "I love the way you two walk," she said. "But I'm curious. How do you keep from falling down?"

Mark chuckled. "It's taken years of practice."

"But it isn't hard," said Liz. "Want to try it?"

"Not me," said their teacher. "I'm too used to doing things the normal way to want to try new tricks. But maybe you two would like to teach the rest of the class tomorrow. I think they'd find it great fun. Would you like to give lessons?"

Mark and Liz grinned at each other. "We'd love to!" they said at the same time.

Smiling and laughing, they ran all the way home—frontward.

Upside-down Cake

"Guess what, Mom and Dad!" Mark said as soon as he and Liz got in the house. "Some of the kids at school like the way we wear our clothes."

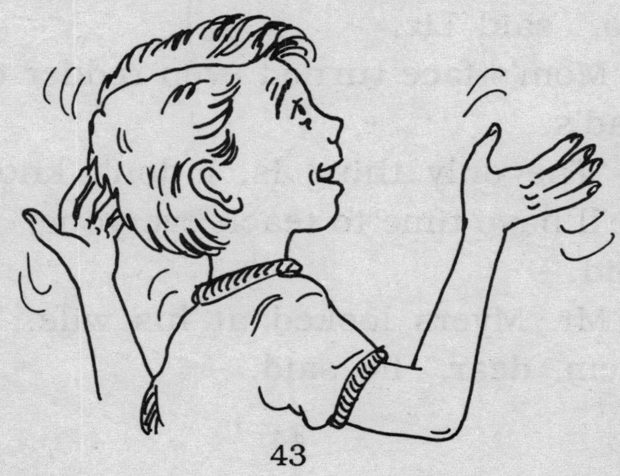

"And our teacher wants us to give the class lessons in walking frontward," Liz added. "We're starting tomorrow."

"Hmm," Mom said. I wonder if that would work for me. I could offer to teach the members of my bulc koob how to walk frontward."

"Your what?" asked Liz.

"My book club," said Mom. She grinned.

"I'd like to teach the men at my office," Dad said. "If they're willing to learn, then I could walk frontward, too."

"Then you could go into the bakery again," Mark said. "Right, Dad?"

Dad's face turned red.

"We could all go to the movies again, too," said Liz.

Mom's face turned even redder than Dad's.

"The only thing is, I don't know if we'll have time to teach everyone," Dad said.

Mr. Myers looked at his wife. "Tell them, dear," he said.

Liz and Mark looked at each other.
Then they looked at Mom.

Their mother smiled and held out a letter she'd received just that day. "Remember my Aunt Kate who died last year? We just found out she left us her big old house in—"

Liz let out a wail before Mom could finish what she was saying. "You want us to leave Drawkcab? We're just getting used to it here. The people in Drawkcab are even getting used to us."

"And we've just learned to be ourselves again," Mark said.

"Well," Mom said, "I guess we could stay here and sell Aunt Kate's house in Upside-down Town."

"Upside-down Town?" said Mark. "That's where Aunt Kate's house is?" He laughed and tried to stand on his head.

"Upside-down Town?" Liz repeated. She giggled and walked across the room on her hands.

"You know what?" said Mark. "Maybe we should keep the house in Upside-down Town for a while."

"In case we change our minds," Liz said.

"How about some upside-down cake right about now?" Mom asked.

"Count me out," said Dad. "I want my meal first and my dessert last. And I want my cake right side up!"

Mark and Liz laughed so hard they got the spuccih.